Love to Leah
from Mommy
&
Daddy
xxxx

Xmas
1991

The Shy Ostrich

by June Woodman

Illustrated by Ken Morton

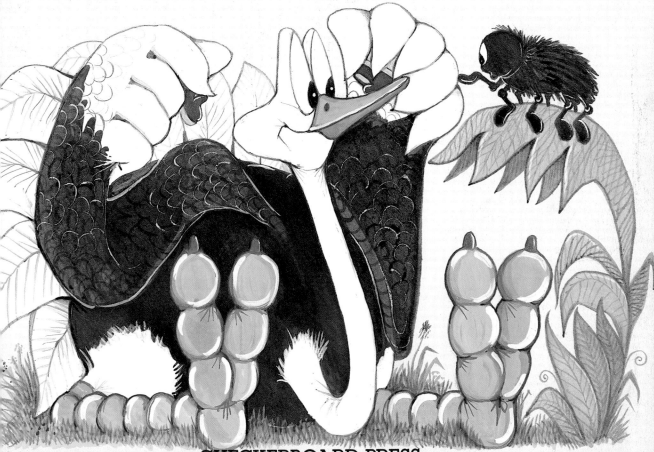

CHECKERBOARD PRESS
NEW YORK

The animals are playing bat and ball. The bat is a branch. The ball is a coconut. Elephant likes to bat. All the animals enjoy playing.
All except Ostrich.
"Come on, Ostrich! Join in the game," calls Kangaroo.
But Ostrich goes red and puts her bucket over her head.
She is too shy to join in.

Ostrich wanders off by herself. Soon she bumps into the trees in Elephant's orange grove. She hears a noise and takes the bucket off her head. She sees Monkey taking Elephant's oranges. Ostrich wants to stop him but she is too shy.

"What shall I do?" she whispers to herself. Then she thinks of something.

Ostrich puts her head in the bucket and makes a loud noise. "Oooeraaah!" she booms.
It sounds just like Elephant.
"Elephant is coming!" cries Monkey. He drops the oranges and scampers off. Ostrich picks up the oranges.
"Put them down!" says a big voice. Elephant has come back. "Why are you taking my oranges?" he shouts crossly.

Ostrich tries to explain.
"I . . . I . . . Oh dear."
She is too shy. She puts her
bucket over her head
and runs off.
Elephant picks up his oranges.
"Stupid bird," he says.
Ostrich keeps running until
she reaches Spider's house.
She hears Monkey again.
He is filling Spider's shoes
with stones.

"What shall I do?" whispers Ostrich to herself.
Then she thinks of something. She finds a stick and picks up her bucket. She taps on her bucket with the stick. Faster and faster she taps. It sounds like Spider.
"Spider is coming," yells Monkey. He drops the shoes and runs away.

Ostrich starts to empty Spider's shoes. Just then Spider appears.
"Hey Ostrich. What are you doing with my shoes?" he asks. Poor Ostrich tries to explain.
"I . . . I . . . Oh dear." She is too shy. She puts her bucket over her head and runs away.
"Funny bird," says Spider.

Ostrich slows down as she reaches Kangaroo's home. She takes the bucket off. She sees Monkey again. He is messing up Baby Kangaroo's toys.
"What shall I do?" whispers Ostrich. Then she thinks of something.

She picks a berry and she draws two eyes and a nose on her bucket. She puts vines on top for the hair. She finds a chalky stone and draws a big, scary mouth. She puts the bucket on her head and stands up in the long grass.

"Whoo! Whoo! WHOOO!"
shouts Ostrich.
Monkey looks up.
He sees a scary face
in the long grass.
"HELP, A MONSTER!"
he screams. He drops the toys
and runs for his life.
Ostrich takes off her bucket
and begins to pick up all the
toys. Then she hears a noise.

Someone is coming along the path. It is Kangaroo.

"Oh, Ostrich," she says. "What are you doing with Baby's toys?"

"I . . . I . . . Oh dear." Ostrich is too shy to explain. She hides in her bucket and runs off. Kangaroo picks up the toys. "Strange bird," she says.

Ostrich sits down and she begins to cry into her bucket. "I . . . I . . . I never took Elephant's oranges. I never put stones in Spider's shoes. I never played with Baby Kangaroo's toys."

"I know, I know," says a voice. It is Parrot.

"I saw it all. I saw it all. It was Monkey. It was Monkey." Parrot likes to say things twice.

"I told everyone. I told everyone," says Parrot. Here they all come now. Monkey is with them. He looks very sad. "He tried to tickle Lion while he was asleep," explains Mouse. "If you promise to be a good Monkey, we will let you go," says Kangaroo. "I promise," says Monkey and he runs away.

"We must have a party for Ostrich," says Kangaroo. "She is such a clever bird." So they have a party. They all sing and dance. Everyone joins in the fun. All except Ostrich. She sits in a corner with her head in her bucket. She is so shy.

Here are some words in the story.

join	booms
game	scampers
grove	stick
hears	yells
noise	scary
taking	monster
whispers	clever